Unicorn Stories

The Flying Unicorn races with the Eagle

Jan Rylewicz

Om KIDZ
An imprint of Om Books International

Dazzle, the unicorn, loved adventures. She flew elegantly and fast with her unicorn friends in the skies. They played all day long in the mystical Fantasy Forest. When she looked down from high above, she could see the lush green Earth full of beautiful flowers, trees, and strange moving creatures, who seemed to be having a lot of fun!

Dazzle wanted to find new friends on Earth. One day, she flew near the fields close to the earthlings.

Dazzle hid behind a tall tree and watched the children kick a small object around. They seemed to be having a jolly good time!

Unknown to Dazzle, a hungry bald eagle called Marcus was sizing her up from the sky above.

As he swooped down towards Dazzle, a soccer ball came flying out of the blue and hit him on his head.

Joey, one of the children playing on the field below, had kicked the ball high up. Marcus the eagle let out an angry squawk, and stopped in its flight, momentarily.

Now Dazzle looked up and saw Marcus. His head gleamed white in contrast to his chocolate-brown body and wings, his eyes were sharp and piercing. Dazzle was frightened. She flew off in the other direction. One of the children, Macy, who was watching Dazzle and Marcus, shouted, “Leave the unicorn alone.” But Marcus was in a naughty mood.

Dazzle needed to rest. But the scary bird was getting closer. "I have to find a way to hide." Yet a beautiful unicorn with flowing purple-coloured hair and shiny yellow horn on her forehead, could not hide that easily.

She had an idea. Maybe the children could help her hide. She landed gently among them. They all stared at her in awe. Dazzle yelled, "Help me hide from that horrid eagle!"

Courtney asked Macy, “Is the unicorn actually talking to us?” But Macy knew there was no time for surprise. Dazzle needed help now, before the eagle swooped down on her!

She jumped on the unicorn’s back and up they went with the eagle in pursuit. Luckily, trees with widespread branches and leaves protected Macy and Dazzle. But Marcus didn’t give up easily!

“Don’t worry, I have a plan,” said Macy, smiling at her fabulous friend. “Let’s hide in a cave by the lake.”

Macy said confidently, “I will get off and stand next to the cave. You will gallop around the lake then dash into the cave. I will close the entrance with a big stone. The eagle won’t be able to see you and fly off.”

Marcus had been following Dazzle closely. But he was confused when he saw the small girl by the lake alone. The plan worked! One moment he could see Dazzle, then suddenly, not anymore! Now Dazzle and Macy were safely hidden in the dark cave.

"Time to give up," he grunted, flying away.

Inside the cave the unicorn said, "My name is Dazzle. Thank you for saving my life. I will come back to play with you and your friends."

Macy was happy to have a new best friend. She pushed the stone from the entrance and checked that Marcus had gone. It was safe to come out.

Macy watched Dazzle fly off into the evening sky. She admired her beautiful rainbow mane and flapping white wings. Suddenly, Dazzle was on the edge. She spied Marcus far away in the sky, hiding behind a fluffy cloud. She did not want to get into a fight with Marcus.

Lost in thoughts, Dazzle suddenly felt a breath of hot air on her mane. Marcus was almost on her. The bully wanted to play more mean games with Dazzle to scare her. "Did you think you could escape me so easily," Marcus scoffed. He pulled Dazzle's beautiful mane.

But all was not lost. Out of the clouds flew Dazzle's mother and father, followed by her unicorn friends. They surrounded Marcus. "Go away, Marcus, you bullying brat," they shouted together. Marcus let go of Dazzle's mane and in his confusion crashed into a towering top of a tree and tumbled, in a mass of ruffled feathers and wings. Marcus had learnt his lesson.

Now Dazzle was finally free! She was happy to be surrounded by her parents and friends. She could hardly believe her eyes!

Dazzle's mother Glitter explained, "Your friends could not find you in Fantasy Forest and were worried. Dolly said you wanted to make friends with human beings! So, we decided to fly down to Earth to find you."

Dazzle smiled, “Thank you all for rescuing me! But I must tell you that the humans are not bad. In fact, a lovely girl called Macy saved my life!”

“You better take us with you when you decide to visit the good humans again!” Dolly said with a smile. Dazzle laughed.

From now on , she often played with the children.